# Lift Off

## by

## Hazel Townson

## Illustrated by Philippe Dupasquier

You do not need to read this page - just get on with the book!

Published in 2002 in Great Britain by
Barrington Stoke Ltd
10 Belford Terrace, Edinburgh EH4 3DQ

This edition based on *Lift Off*, published by Barrington Stoke in 1999

Printed by Polestar Ltd, Aberdeen

## Meet The Author - Hazel Townson

*What is your favourite animal?*
A dog
*What is your favourite boy's name?*
Christopher
*What is your favourite girl's name?*
Catherine
*What is your favourite food?*
Strawberries
*What is your favourite music?*
Classical, especially Mahler
*What is your favourite hobby?*
Table tennis

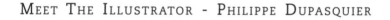

## Meet The Illustrator - Philippe Dupasquier

*What is your favourite animal?*
A tiger
*What is your favourite boy's name?*
Jonathan
*What is your favourite girl's name?*
Sophie
*What is your favourite food?*
Oysters
*What is your favourite music?*
Rock music
*What is your favourite hobby?*
Drawing

For Sue Stephenson, a great
champion of children's books

# Contents

# Chapter 1
# A Terrible Mistake

Ronnie hated all sport. It was kids' stuff.
He knew he could kick, catch, run or jump
better than anyone else, but why bother?
It was all too much like hard work. Let the
others rush about after a ball and limp
home with mud all over them. It was more
fun to watch the telly any day.

If anyone had said he was lazy he would just have grinned. Let them think that. Ronnie knew he wasn't lazy – he was just wise. After all, *he* didn't limp home, wet and worn out.

Tuesdays and Fridays were Ronnie's bad days, because there was sport all afternoon. But he found a lot of good excuses not to join in. He had a bad back, or hay fever or a trip to the dentist.

But there was one thing Ronnie could not get out of, and that was Sports Day.

No-one could get out of Sports Day. The Head, Mr Borden, had said that every child must join in. There was always a relay race or a tug-of-war for the 'duds'. That was where Ronnie ended up because he'd missed so much.

But not this year!

When Ronnie looked down the lists for Sports Day, he was amazed to find he had nothing to do. His name was not down on any list.

A new sports teacher had just joined the school. His name was Mr Springer. He was still learning what was what when Sports Day came round. He had to draw up the lists in such a hurry that Ronnie's name was left out.

How lucky could you be? Ronnie knew he should tell Mr Springer, but he wasn't going to.

He thought no-one would find out that he was not on the lists. He would flop about in his PE kit and look as if he had just run a race. Everyone would be far too busy to find out the truth. People said that the Head had so much work to do that he might not come at all.

Never trust what people say! The Head was not going to miss Sports Day. He knew the names of all his pupils. Three days before Sports Day, the Head looked down

the lists with Mr Springer. He saw at once that Ronnie's name was missing.

"Didn't young Ronnie come and tell you that he wasn't on any list?" the Head asked Mr Springer. "He knows quite well that everyone joins in on Sports Day. Everyone!"

"Er – he hasn't said anything to me yet!" replied Mr Springer.

The Head frowned. "Well, he's had lots of time to do so. I bet he's trying to get out of it. That lad's for the high jump."

What the Head meant was that he was going to give Ronnie a hard time. But Mr Springer thought that the Head had told him to put Ronnie's name down to do the high jump.

Things were looking bad for Ronnie, as bad as they could be.

# Chapter 2
## One Jump Ahead

When Mr Springer told Ronnie he must do the high jump, the poor lad could not hide his shock.

"But sir, I can't jump! I've got this funny heel," he said.

Mr Springer looked hard at Ronnie's feet.

"You look OK to me. Have you ever tried to jump?" he asked.

"Well, no, sir. But I'd be no good. I'm not that sort, sir."

If the Head thinks you can do it, then you have to try," Springer told him. "Meet me at the Sports ground at 8:30 am tomorrow, then again after school. I'll try you out."

Ronnie looked cross. The high jump was no joke. In fact, it was *very* hard work. He'd have to train for it. What a bore!

"I can't get to school for 8:30. My bus doesn't get here till 8:50."

"Then you'll have to walk or catch a bus that *does* get here on time."

"Sir, Mum won't let me walk in case I get run over," Ronnie told him.

"Oh, come on now! Your mum will be proud that you are in the team. And *you* should be proud that the Head thinks you can do it. You don't want to let us all down, do you? You be there at 8:30 tomorrow. That's an order."

"Yes, sir!"

But when Mr Springer saw that Ronnie was looking upset, he added, "You don't know what you can do until you try. And I'll be there to help you."

This was the worst day of Ronnie's life. He'd been found out at last. The poor lad got home feeling sick about the whole thing. The boys in his class would think it was the best joke ever.

Even worse, if his parents found out he was in the high jump final, they would come to Sports Day!

His parents were not back from work yet. Ronnie let himself in to the empty house with the key he kept on a string round his neck. How could he get out of this bad dream? He felt ill.

*Ill?*

Then he knew what he had to do. He would stay off school the next day!

He would be ill. And the next day. And the day after that, which was Sports Day. He could write out a sick note for his teacher in his mum's handwriting.

He felt fine now. Why hadn't he thought of this before? He had never bunked off school like the others. Why not now?

He began to make plans. He would set out for school, but would miss the bus. But he had better not hang about the streets. His dad did a van round and might zoom past at any moment. Better to slip home after his mum and dad had left for work.

I've cracked it, thought Ronnie feeling happy again.

How wrong he was.

# Chapter 3
# Enter – A Murderer!

Next day, Ronnie got ready for school as he always did.

"Watch out for the traffic, love!" his mother warned him as she dashed off to work.

"Come on, son, I'll give you a lift," joked Ronnie's dad as he started up the van.

He knew that Ronnie would rather die than be seen going to school with his dad.

Ronnie waved goodbye and trotted off. On the way to the bus stop he hid in a shop doorway for a time. As soon as he felt safe, he dashed back home and let himself in. No-one had seen him.

He would hide up in his bedroom. No-one could see in from outside. He had a desk up there. He could work on his Save the Earth project for school.

But before he could start on the project, he must write the sick note. He tried again and again to write like his mum, but it didn't work. He tore all the notes into tiny shreds.

Then he had an idea. He found his mum's shopping list. Now he could copy the way she did each letter.

After that, he began to get bored. The morning dragged on and he began to feel hungry. He crept down to the kitchen.

The first thing he saw on the kitchen
table was his dad's newspaper. It said in
big, black letters on the front page,
BURGLAR KIDNAPS BOY. Ronnie snatched up
the paper and began to read.

The boy in the story was called Sam. He
lived in the very next town. That made the
story even better.

While Sam's parents were out, Sam had come home to find a burglar in the house. The burglar had grabbed Sam and driven away with him in a green Land Rover.

Sam had not been seen since. The police had looked everywhere, even in the river. There were fears that Sam was dead.

Had the burglar been found? Ronnie wanted to read on and find out, but just then there was a lot of noise outside the front door.

Thump, drag, thump, drag.

He put down the newspaper to listen. It was too late for the postman, so what could it be?

Ronnie waited for the bell to ring. Horror of horrors – it could even be someone from school!

It was even worse than that. Ronnie could now hear a key turn in the lock. Someone was coming in!

Ronnie was in a panic. It must be one of his parents. Well, they had better not find him at home. Quick as a blink, he hid in the cubby-hole under the stairs where the boots were kept.

For a time, he stood in the dark among the boots and listened. Someone was tramping up and down the hall, making a lot of noise. It didn't sound like his mum or dad.

In the end he had to know who it was. He opened the cubby-hole door a crack and looked out.

He was just in time to see a man walking off down the hall with the TV set. And it wasn't his dad. Beyond the open front door, Ronnie saw a green Land Rover. It was parked right outside the house.

A green Land Rover!

What had it said in the newspaper? The burglar who went off with Sam had a green Land Rover. This man in the hall, this burglar who was taking their TV, must be the same one. He might kidnap Ronnie too if he saw him!

*I could end up in the river – dead!* thought Ronnie.

He felt sick and dizzy. He fell against the cubby-hole door and it swung open with a crash. The burglar turned round – and the two of them came face to face.

Better to face the high jump than this burglar. Ronnie thought he would remember this moment for the rest of his life – if he still had a life.

The burglar had not got a mask over his face. This scared Ronnie. The man must be sure he would get away with it. If anyone saw him they would think he was taking the TV to mend it. They would not phone the police or rush to help Ronnie. Even though Ronnie might soon be dead.

*Now the burglar knows that I have seen his face*, thought Ronnie.

He knows I'll remember it too. How can I ever forget it? It makes me enemy number one! He'll have to shut me up, just as he did with Sam!

Ronnie crashed out of the back door and fled.

# Chapter 4
# No Hiding Place

Ronnie was sure the burglar would follow him. The burglar did have his arms full with the TV but he would soon get rid of that. Then he could give chase in that green Land Rover.

Better keep off the roads. Ronnie dived down a lane and on into the park.

OK so far, but he couldn't stay in the park all day. He was not keen to go and tell

his parents or the police. If he did, they'd find out that he hadn't been to school.

There must be some place that was safe to hide until the end of the school day. Then he could go home late. He would make sure that he arrived *after* his mum. He wanted *her* to find out that the TV had gone.

By that time, thought Ronnie, the burglar will know that I've not told on him. So he won't need to murder me after all.

But where could he hide right now? He would have to find a good place. It was a matter of life or death.

Then Ronnie thought of something he had learnt at school. If you hid in a church, no-one would come and get you. He ran over to St Steven's but the church door was locked. *Just my bad luck!* thought Ronnie.

He turned away. Then he saw the library close by the church. He would try in there. No-one got murdered in a library.

The children's library was always busy when Ronnie went there after school. Now it was almost empty.

Mrs Oates, the library lady, was at her desk. Ronnie could see that she had her eye on him. He fled to the back of the room, grabbed any old book and began to read.

That did not stop Mrs Oates from coming over to talk to him. "Why aren't you in school?" she asked.

"I'm – er – doing my project on Save the Earth," Ronnie told her.

Mrs Oates looked at his book. "Well, you won't get much help from a book on ballet dancing."

Ronnie blushed and said nothing. He was bad at lying.

"Has your teacher sent you here?" asked Mrs Oates.

"We – er – I have to find things out for myself," Ronnie told her. He knew now that it had been a mistake to come in here. He put the book on a shelf, and ran out of the door.

*Now* where should he go? It was raining hard. Blame Sports Day! Blame Mr Springer and the Head! They were the ones who had got him into this mess.

# Chapter 5
# One Shock After Another!

The rain was pouring down by now and Ronnie needed to find shelter.

He *could* go to the shopping centre. At other times Ronnie loved going there. He liked hunting for dropped coins. He had once found 17 pence in a single day!

But the shopping centre was a long way away. It was near the school too. Ronnie

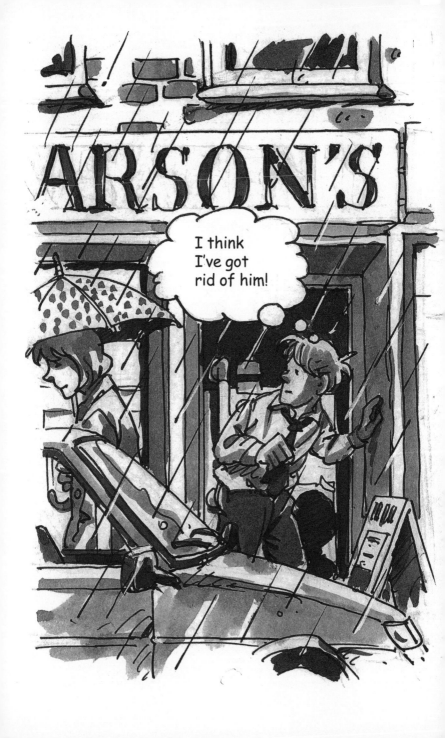

was still in a panic that someone might spot him. He hid in one shop doorway after another. He kept looking back but saw no sign of a green Land Rover.

By the time he came to the shopping centre he was sure the burglar had lost track of him.

Whew!

Ronnie was so wet that he had to prop himself against a heater in the toy shop to get dry. He still felt shaky, but safe and much more hopeful. A Land Rover could not drive in here.

He began to think of himself as a bit of a hero. After all, he had escaped from a burglar who wanted to kill him.

*Life isn't over yet,* Ronnie thought.

He began to look around him. Right in front of him, he saw a new type of model bus.

Ronnie was keen on model buses. He picked it up. Ronnie was just looking at the price to see how long it would take him to save up for it, when someone grabbed hold of him.

"Now then," said the owner of the shop, "I've been watching you. About to nick that bus, were you? Well, get back to school."

What a shock! For one moment Ronnie thought it was the burglar who had grabbed him. The owner thought he was going to steal this bus. He had never nicked anything. He had only picked up lost coins and that was not at all the same thing.

"I was only looking ..." he began.

"That's what they all say. Got any money?"

"I've got my bus fare ..."

"Well, you come back in the school holidays with your pocket money and you can have a good look then."

The owner took the bus from Ronnie and pushed him out of the shop. Ronnie ran off. What an insult! The shame of it.

"Here, look where you're going!" a woman yelled as he ran right into her.

"Kids!" said her friend in disgust. "No manners at all! And anyway, why isn't he in school?"

Ronnie started running again. One of these bossy people might make him go back to school. Then all at once he spotted his dad's TV set. A man was just putting it in a shop window. Ronnie stopped and looked at the sign above the window. It said, GET YOUR ALMOST-NEW TVs, VIDEOS AND RADIOS HERE.

Ronnie looked hard at the TV set. He knew it was his dad's because it had a scratch on its side.

So the burglar *had* come into the shopping centre! Perhaps he was here right now, waiting to grab him?

Ronnie looked around in panic. The place was packed with people. Ronnie had thought he could never forget the burglar's face. But he knew now that any of the men around him could be the burglar.

That was it! He would have to tell the police while the TV was still in the window. If he waited, the TV might be sold. Then no-one would believe his story.

He had seen a phone box near the toy shop. He could dial 999 for free. He spun round to run back to it – and came face to face with the burglar who was just coming out of the TV shop.

# Chapter 6
# A Leap for Dear Life

Ronnie had never run so fast in his life. He dashed at speed in and out of all the people. It was amazing what you could do when your life was at risk.

From time to time he saw the burglar's reflection in a shop window. This made him run even faster. Soon he was outside the shopping centre again and rushing down Hill Street towards school.

Towards school?

He no longer cared about being found out. School was the safest place to be. Even the Head would not stand by and watch him being killed. Ronnie had to go there as soon as he could.

Hill Street was steep and the school was at the bottom, with playing fields all round it. The ground was wet and slippery from the rain.

Ronnie began to run faster and faster. As he shot down the hill it became clear that he could not stop himself.

What could he do?

There was a high hedge all the way round the playing fields. There were two gates in the hedge, but they were a long way off. Ronnie found himself rushing straight towards the hedge!

That hedge was about a metre and a half high – but Ronnie did a great leap and flew right over it. He landed on the grass of the playing field a few metres from Mr Springer, the Sports master. Mr Springer was amazed.

"I know I told you to train, Ronnie, but I didn't think you would risk your neck by jumping over the hedge," he said.

Ronnie lay panting on the grass. He could not even reply. Mr Springer rushed over to see if the boy was hurt. Once he was sure Ronnie was OK, he helped him to his feet.

"Well, now we know that you can jump as well as anyone and better than most," Mr Springer said. "I'm sorry you didn't get to school this morning as we planned. And don't jump any more hedges!"

If anyone could save Ronnie now, it was Mr Springer. Ronnie took a deep breath and told his story.

"Sir, someone is trying to kill me! He's been chasing me all round the shopping centre. That's why I jumped over the hedge."

"Tut, tut," said Mr Springer. "Well, that's the most odd excuse for a morning off that I've ever heard."

"Honest, Sir, he stole our TV and I saw. That's why he's chasing me. He's already killed a boy called Sam."

"Well, I think you stayed away from school to miss the high jump training. So no more stories from you. And you'd better turn up for training after school today, my lad. You're a born high jumper."

"But Sir ...!"

"Don't say another word, Ronnie. Get back to your classroom and be thankful that I'm not going to pass on your silly story to the Head."

Ronnie groaned.

# Chapter 7
# A Big Surprise

Ronnie crossed the playing field to go up to his classroom. He did not hurry. He needed time to think up a good excuse.

All at once he spotted a van outside the gym door. It was his dad's van! His dad was bringing some new benches for the school.

Ronnie started to run.

"Dad! Dad! Wait for me!" he yelled, as his father walked back to his van.

Here at last was someone who would believe Ronnie's story, even if it did land him in a mess.

"There was a burglar at home, Dad! And he is trying to kill me!" Ronnie told his dad.

"What did you say?" his dad laughed.

"It's true, Dad!"

Ronnie's Dad could see that his son was most upset. He put an arm round him.

"OK, just calm down and take it slowly, son. Who's been burgled? Your class?"

"No, we have! Us. Our family. *Our* house! This burglar's nicked our telly, and he has a green Land Rover so he could have killed me. It says so in your paper."

"Slow up a bit!"

Ronnie's Dad began to laugh again.
"If you mean Jack Briggs, he's taken our old
TV and given us a new one. It was going to
be a surprise for Mum and you. Wait till
you see it! Teletext, cable and the lot. You'll
love it. I gave Jack a key to the house so he

could slip it in before Mum and you got home."

Dad looked puzzled. "Wait a moment. How did you know about it anyway? You were at school."

*Here it comes*, thought Ronnie. But his father was going to find out anyway. So he told him the whole story.

"But how could I know that he wasn't out to kill me? He was chasing me, Dad!"

"He must have seen how scared you were and wanted to tell you who he was. Or he thought YOU were a burglar, when you ran off like that."

Ronnie found it hard to take all this in. He felt angry. Someone had made a fool of him.

But there was one good thing about all this. His dad could see he was in no fit state to train for Sports Day. He would see to it that Ronnie did not have to.

No such luck! Mr Springer came over just then to see why Ronnie hadn't gone back into school.

Dad had to tell him who he was. He also told Mr Springer what Ronnie had just told him.

"He got it all wrong," his dad said, "but you can see the boy's upset."

Mr Springer did not say that if Ronnie had come to school this morning, all this would never have happened. He was too pleased to find out that Ronnie was a star at the high jump. He told Dad how Ronnie had come racing down the hill and how he had jumped over the hedge.

"It was one of the best jumps I've ever seen. And with a bit of training, he'll do even better."

Ronnie's dad grinned. "I always knew he had it in him," he said with pride. "Just wait till I tell his mum that Ronnie may win the high jump on Sports Day."

"But Dad, look how upset I am! You can't let me train now," yelled Ronnie in a panic.

His dad did not seem to hear. He was thinking of the moment when Ronnie would win the high jump.

Then he had an idea.

"Tell you what! As Ronnie ran down that hill so fast, why don't you put him in for the 100 metre race as well?"

# Who is Barrington Stoke?

Barrington Stoke went from place to place with his lamp in his hand. Everywhere he went, he told stories to children. Some were happy, some were sad, some were funny and some were scary.

The children always wanted more. When it got dark, they had to go home to bed. They went to look for Barrington Stoke the next day, but he had gone.

The children never forgot the stories. They told them to each other and to their children and their grandchildren. You see, good stories are magic and they can live forever.

**If you loved this story, why don't you read ...**

# Problems with a Python

## by Jeremy Strong

Have you ever looked after a friend's pet? Adam agrees to look after a friend's pet python, but things get wildly out of hand!

You can order this book directly from
Macmillan Distribution Ltd, Brunel Road, Houndmills,
Basingstoke, Hampshire RG21 6XS   Tel: 01256 302699